蔡榮勇 著
戴茉莉 譯
Poems by Tsai Jung-yung
Translated by Emily Anna Deasy

I am Literate

蔡榮勇漢英雙語詩集
Mandarin - English

台灣詩叢 • Taiwan Poetry Series 25

【總序】詩推台灣印象

叢書策劃／李魁賢

　　進入21世紀，台灣詩人更積極走向國際，個人竭盡所能，在詩人朋友熱烈參與支持下，策畫出席過印度、蒙古、古巴、智利、緬甸、孟加拉、尼加拉瓜、馬其頓、秘魯、突尼西亞、越南、希臘、羅馬尼亞、墨西哥等國舉辦的國際詩歌節，並編輯《台灣心聲》等多種詩選在各國發行，使台灣詩人心聲透過作品傳佈國際間。

　　多年來進行國際詩交流活動最困擾的問題，莫如臨時編輯帶往國外交流的選集，大都應急處理，不但時間緊迫，且選用作品難免會有不周。因此，興起策畫【台灣詩叢】雙語詩系的念頭。若台灣詩人平常就有雙語詩集出版，隨時可以應用，詩作交流與詩人交誼雙管齊下，更具實際成效，對台灣詩的國際交流活動，當更加順利。

　　以【台灣】為名，著眼點當然有鑑於台灣文學在國際間名目不彰，台灣詩人能夠有機會在國際努力開拓空間，非為個人建立知名度，而是為推展台灣意象的整體事功，期待開創台灣文學的長久景象，才能奠定寶貴的歷史意義，台灣文學終必在世界文壇上佔有地位。

實際經驗也明顯印證，台灣詩人參與國際詩交流活動，很受重視，帶出去的詩選集也深受歡迎，從近年外國詩人和出版社與本人合作編譯台灣詩選，甚至主動翻譯本人詩集在各國文學雜誌或詩刊發表，進而出版外譯詩集的情況，大為增多，即可充分證明。

　　承蒙秀威資訊科技公司一本支援詩集出版初衷，慨然接受【台灣詩叢】列入編輯計畫，對台灣詩的國際交流，提供推進力量，希望能有更多各種不同外語的雙語詩集出版，形成進軍國際的集結基地。

【自序】

　　感謝詩人林鷺的推介,也感謝翻譯家Emily的翻譯。

　　感謝不識字的阿爸、阿母,讓我讀書識字,會寫詩是這我輩子感到最幸福的事情。

　　女兒Sherrie,29歲那一年,就移民到天堂。想要跟她聊天,僅僅透過禱告。

　　李白的名句:「舉頭望明月,低頭思故鄉。」望月,我不是思鄉,乃是孤寂的思念。低頭想念女兒,不禁舉頭望明月,然而明月懂得我心中的傷悲嗎?

　　女兒是我心中種植的一株仙人掌,有意無意刺痛著心,每當刺了一下,就得趕緊寫一首詩止血,否則血流不停。

　　最後感謝吳霽恆編輯和秀威資訊團隊的合作幫忙,也要感謝太太讓我任性的寫詩。

2025.04.24　一稿

我識字
I am Literate

女兒 Sherrie

目次
CONTENTS

目次

- 3 【總序】詩推台灣印象／李魁賢
- 5 【自序】

- 9 　我識字・I am Literate
- 13 　禱告・Prayer
- 14 　台灣的心事・Sentiments of Taiwan
- 15 　洗衣婦・Washer Woman
- 16 　五分車・Sugarcane Trains
- 18 　我還在學・I Am Still Learning
- 20 　芳苑海邊・The Fangyuan Seaside
- 21 　許久　許久・A Long Time A Long Time
- 23 　天主教堂・Catholic Church
- 24 　媽祖廟・Mazu Temple
- 25 　讀・Read
- 27 　不識字的母親・Illiterate Mother
- 28 　萬仔！萬仔！・Father's Name
- 29 　賣雞販・Chicken Vendor
- 31 　我比阿爸幸福・I Am More Fortunate Than Father
- 33 　靜下心來・Silencing the Heart
- 35 　鞋・Shoes
- 36 　台灣精神・Taiwan Spirit
- 37 　尷尬・Awkward

38	誰當裁判	Who Will Be the Referee
40	自畫像	Self-portrait
41	太陽花	Sunflower
43	洗衣婦	The Washerwoman
45	剩下她自己	With Only Herself Left
47	悲慟的聽覺	The Auditory Sense of Grief
55	給女兒詩穎	For My Daughter Sherrie
60	為女兒禱告	Praying for My Daughter
61	蠶	Silkworms
63	國家大事	Major National Affairs
65	吾鄉北斗	My Hometown Beidou
67	風景	Landscape
68	作者簡介	About the Poet
69	譯者簡介	About the Translator

我識字

父親失去父親
很小很小的時候
沒有品嘗到上學的滋味

父親睜亮生活的眼睛
依靠雙手雙腳
養育我們長大

我識字
我才知道父親
在國民黨的國語優勢下
自卑、畏縮，躲在牆角過日子

我識字
我才知道父親
被貼上貧窮
這一餐有飯吃趕緊快樂
下一餐再煩惱

我識字
I am Literate

我識字
也不能掙脫國民黨
統治的高傲
仍然一餐苦過一餐
不敢有太陽、月亮的空隙

我識字
也讓孩子學英語、日語
讓眼睛伸出台灣海峽
她坐在英國大學的教室
上課

我識字
孩子生病了
眼睜睜看著她上天堂
我的雙手萎縮，心靈也乾裂
日子是失焦的影像

我識字
也看不見上帝
真想對上帝說
女兒,是我一輩子的
希望

好不容易
在國民黨統治下的岩石
開出了一朵小黃花
還來不及,在風中展靨
就將她吹落了

我識字
卻找不到,可以
坐到天堂的飛機
用詩刷洗哀愁
越是哀愁

我識字
I am Literate

我識字
世界還是一樣
留不下我
任何的腳印
一片飄落的枯葉

禱告

沙洲上站著
一排排的水鳥
默默的禱告
「肚子餓時,可以
　吃到新鮮的小魚」

一聲阿們

鼓動翅膀
降落水面
咬起小魚
縮著單腳睡覺
迎接黑夜的好夢

我識字
I am Literate

台灣的心事

不能叫自己國家的名字
台灣

不能閱讀祖先留下來的
文化

不能用阿母講的話
讀　說　寫　作
叫我們要　如　何
高
　　瞻
　　　　遠
　　　　　　矚

洗衣婦

天空張開惺忪的眼睛
趕緊趕路　脫下
青春典當給髒衣服
連同心靈也一併
典押下去

一湯匙的洗衣粉
一臉盆的溼衣服
等待　風的呼喚
等待　陽光的情書
等待　鈔票的恩典

手指頭　過勞
張開狗嘴巴
學閃電　SOS
我不要貧窮
我不要貧窮

我識字
I am Literate

五分車

每次返鄉　坐火車
只能坐到員林
再轉台汽客運回北斗
眼睛不禁轉向
小時候的五分車
家門前就是驛站北勢寮

每當火車進站時
聽到ㄅㄨㄅㄨㄅㄨ的汽笛聲
那是載甘蔗的火車
聽到咻一聲
那是載客人的火車

現在台糖製糖沒落了
廢除五分車，連同車站也賣了
夷為平地，大家爭相搶購
蓋起違章建築出租

家鄉的感覺
就像眼前的雜草
寂寞‧孤單

我識字
I am Literate

我還在學

一叢綠色的秧苗
日頭下
面不改綠

一叢綠色的秧苗
日頭下
綠色臉孔

一叢綠色的秧苗
日頭下
綠色笑容

一叢綠色的秧苗
日頭下
搜尋綠色成語

查累了
日頭熱熱的說
該休息了

秋風，買了
一本新的成語辭典
送給秧苗

秧苗客氣的說
我還在學
謝謝你

我識字
I am Literate

芳苑海邊

芳苑海邊的沙灘是條平靜空曠
泥濘漿漿的鄉間小路
一隻黃牛穿過海風的心靈
以一種垂直的平行拖著牛車
踩著沙灘　一個腳印
一個腳印追逐夕陽

一道比海邊更熟悉的人影
她從夢裡的海邊　經過
凝視的夕陽　餘暉殘影
她貼近我，進入我
躍進到靈魂　金兔銀蟾
的月窗

許久　許久

許久　許久
跟著阿爸祭拜　見過面的祖先
許久　許久
跟著阿爸祭拜　不曾見過面的祖先
許久　許久
跟著阿爸祭拜　阿爸不曾見過面的祖先

祖先祭拜　祖先的身影
祖先的　祖先的身影　祭拜
祭拜　祖先的　祖先的身影

百日後
阿爸也成為祖先的身影
初一、十五　記得要祭拜

看慣了阿爸流汗的眼睛
不習慣阿爸遺照的眼睛
那是一冊歷史的小書

我識字
I am Literate

收藏　阿爸無以數計
的眼睛

手持三支清香
看慣阿爸的眼睛
我的眼睛
膽小也膽怯

列祖列宗
一定有話要說
只是　耳朵聽不到
金紙熊熊的火焰
看到了
阿爸的眼睛
熊熊的火焰似的發亮

天主教堂

走進教堂
右膝長跪
右手輕點十字
坐下來，聆聽
神父親切的台語講道

心情像台灣玉山
靜下來
媽媽責罵的話
像天空的烏雲
飄　走　了

2013/1/17修

我識字
I am Literate

媽祖廟

媽媽心裡有了煩惱
買了幾粒水果
買了一盒餅乾
買了一束香
買了一疊金紙
到了廟裡向媽祖
告白，祈求媽祖
保佑身體健康勢讀冊

回家
我最高興
有水果吃
有餅乾吃

媽媽臉上
還有幾朵烏雲
停在額頭上

讀

僅僅會說幾句國語的
母親
文字的家園
眼睛找不到
鑰匙

工作　天天讀
讀累了　便讀
兒女
讀累了　夢的眼睛
繼續讀
讀累了　便讀兒女的
夢

兒女也寫了一本
她愛讀的書
想　拿出來
拿不出來

我識字
I am Literate

唸給他聽
「太長了」
她說

不識字的母親

不識字的母親
每個人的表情
她感動的詩句

每日的工作
她必讀的散文

和人聊天
她愛讀的小說

愛子女的心
她讀不倦的哲學

她不知道
她是一本子女
愛讀的百科全書

我識字
I am Literate

萬仔！萬仔！

阿爸往生後
阿母雙手拿著兩個五十元銅板
一再的叫喊　阿爸的　小名
「萬仔！萬仔！
我按呢做
你會歡喜嗎？」

失去一個六十年的老伴
阿母的　寂
比北極的冰雪還
冷

子女的貼心
貼不著
阿母的心
僅僅是一塊墜地的翡翠

賣雞販

一雙手
一雙腳
一顆勤勞的心
擔著一家六口的

一台腳踏車載著
一籠雞仔
大街小巷
村頭村尾
吆喝著
「俗擱好吃的土雞」
「俗擱好吃的土雞」

躺在床上　觀看
這樣的影片
眼淚變成蚊子
在耳邊嗡嗡叫

我識字
I am Literate

陽光在窗戶旁亮亮的叫喊
「起床了！」
「日頭照尻川！」
陽光不知道
這樣的觀看有多甜蜜

我比阿爸幸福

1955年出生的我
我比阿爸幸福
阿爸還在我身邊　叮嚀
種植芭蕉　收割芭蕉

沒有父親叮嚀的阿爸
不知道怎樣做父親
往往是石頭的沉默
往往是翠綠的芭蕉葉

阿爸上天堂了
思念比活著更真實
活著會回鄉探望
上天堂路變得更寬廣

我識字
I am Literate

我比阿爸幸福
阿爸陪伴在我身邊　叮嚀
阿爸上天堂
我可以真實的回憶

2019/1/9　修

靜下心來

從明天起　我要離開學校
離開教室　離開操場
離開天真可愛的學生
靜下心來　懷念中師實小

從明天起　我要走向鄉村
跟農夫請教種植水稻的方法
跟麻雀請教觀看水稻成長的心得
靜下心來　懷念中師實小

從明天起　我要走向漁村
跟漁夫請教捕魚的技巧
跟海鷗請教飛行的樂趣
靜下心來　懷念中師實小

我識字
I am Literate

從明天起　我要走向高山
跟原住民請教傾聽寂靜
跟千年神請教沉默孤獨
靜下心來　懷念中師實小

從明天起　我要走向我
走向自己生命的桃花源
跟生命對話甚至爭辯
靜下心來　懷念中師實小

鞋

女人穿鞋
不是為了　寫散文給男人　閱讀
也不是為了　寫故事給男人　閱讀
僅僅是　寫一首小詩給青春閱讀

女人買鞋
可能想要更換男人
或許是想偷情
也許是墜入情網

櫃子上擺放的鞋子
嘴巴　張開Ｏ字形
是累了
還是有話要說

我識字
I am Literate

台灣精神

讀小學　初中　師專的歷史課本都是中國歷史
每一個朝代都是皇帝無能或殘暴另一位
有膽識的人揭竿起義獲勝龍袍上身
好人壞人兩條線把五千年的歷史串聯起來

台灣歷史一再提起鄭成功驅趕荷蘭人
一再歌頌蔣介石多麼的偉大
大陸淪陷的原因　一陣霧

我跟不識字的父母親學習台灣精神
他們一生努力工作待人熱情善良
生活節儉樸素

2001.10.20　一稿
2019.05.09　二稿

尷尬

蔣介石的聖旨
反共抗俄
在手臂　用針寫上
反共抗俄　思念故鄉

李登輝說
解除戒嚴
老兵可以返鄉

手臂上
青綠色的反共抗俄
在手術房　跟瓶子裡的
小花　傾訴
我的故鄉

我識字
I am Literate

誰當裁判

讀國小
老師一再叮嚀
「反共抗俄」

讀初中
老師一再叮嚀
「毋忘在莒」

讀師專
老師一再叮嚀
「處變不驚」

教書時
蔣經國總統說
我也是台灣人

結婚時
李登輝總統頒布
解嚴令

邁入中年
中國結和台灣結
拔河

不知誰來當裁判
是不是爬得高高的
太陽

我識字
I am Literate

自畫像

退休了
不再是老師
走在路上跟行道樹一樣
很少人　會抬頭看你

不會開車
喜歡坐火車看風景
不是有錢人
打打羽球流流汗
偶爾　看看詩集畫冊
偶爾　種種花草樹木
偶爾　寫寫詩畫畫圖

生活
就這樣活著
試著
將心靈深深踩在
養我育我的台灣泥土

2006/11/25修

太陽花

太陽花　喚醒了
百合花學運的精神
尋找台灣存在的窗口

太陽花綻開的花朵
鄭南榕自焚的血花
詹益樺自焚的血花

太陽不畏黑箱的服貿
撐起太陽花
等待天光的日照

太陽花　照亮　宏碁董事長
他說：「服貿不過，台灣產業沒有希望！」

太陽花　照亮　義守集團董事長
他說　他會暫緩在台灣的一切投資。

我識字
I am Literate

太陽花　照亮　台塑董事長
他說　再鬧下去，恐怕15K也領不到！

太陽花　照亮　台達電創辦人
他說　台灣會有邊緣化的危機

太陽花的雲端　驅趕
馬政府的烏賊

太陽花全球性的網路
嚇跑棍棒的對話

2019/4/18　改

洗衣婦

詩人張香華〈一件紅絨衫〉
柔軟的，粗硬的
溫馨，變成嘮叨的叮嚀

詩人朵思〈洗衣〉
志氣是一吋吋的短
愛與關懷卻一截截增多

阿母不是詩人，是〈洗衣婦〉
寒天透早
雙手在洗衣板
為一家家換下的髒衣服
洗乾淨

乾淨寫在裂開的手指頭
滴血

我識字
I am Literate

附記：記得國小五六年級補習費一個月要繳五十元，為了繳納補習費，阿母厚著臉皮跟附近有錢人家洗衣服，一個月也是五十元。每每想到這樣的場景，眼淚找不到躲藏的地方。不懂得同理心的女主人，往往扔下無以數計的衣服讓阿母洗。

剩下她自己

阿母不會說國語
阿母不會說客語
阿母不會說原住民語
阿母不會看報紙
會用眼睛看世界
會用耳朵聽世界
會用心靈讀世界

她的世界,無法透過書籍
穿越她不曾走過的世界

她用母親告訴她的語言
她用眼睛閱讀世界
她不用查字典,因為沒有生字

父親過世了
她更老了
世界越來越小

我識字
I am Literate

剩下她自己
孤　單

2018/2/13
2025/4/16　修

悲慟的聽覺

> 你不是滄海中的一滴水,你是囊括整片海域的水粒子(You are not a drop in the ocean. You are the entire ocean in a drop.)
>
> ——伊斯蘭教詩人盧米(Rumi)

序曲

她成為一則傳說,終於可以像一隻麻雀到處飛翔,找不到可以棲息的樹幹,一不小心墜落在我的悲愴,留下一個深深的凹陷。

A

傾聽,悲慟的聽覺悲慟的
比活著歲月更多的思念
比思念更多活著的歲月
沿著思念回到她的童年
且擦拭鞋子底下的汙泥

我識字
I am Literate

每走一步,偷偷的回頭
一回頭,心靈碎了滿地玻璃
她是最重要的主詞
我到處收集了許多動詞
緩慢地,修補破碎的心靈

每走一步,就得丟棄幾個動詞
抵達童年,一本繪本矗立在前方
醒目的題目,〈你就是一本生命之書〉

她,在生與死兩個字
之間,消失在另一個字
我要用生閱讀死,找尋死亡的居所。

B

死的語言像一隻烏賊
遇到強敵,不斷

吐出黑墨汁,大海的巨肚
一點感覺也沒有,仍然
浪來浪去,漁夫
繼續捕魚,海風
張開巨大的翅膀
咆嘯,漁船且浮且沉
駛向岸邊,漁夫滿船的魚貨
生的單字,一再的被書寫
奔向魚市場,奔向每個
消費者的肚子

死的語言像一棵枯死的神木
長不出
因為根已經腐爛
活著的神木
葉子翠綠
樹幹的皺紋有歲月的皺紋
風吹得動

我識字
I am Literate

小鳥願意來棲息、唱歌

枯死的神木　默默等待
鋸子的切割
做椅子、桌子、雕刻
她死了，三個字
時間記不住
太陽早已忘記了
月亮繼續照亮她的窗戶
她的影子跟月亮一同
床前　明月光　不能
舉頭　望明月

思念她
舉頭看明月

C

她,上天堂了
沿著這句話的蜿蜒
真的假的,相互糾纏的荊棘
樹木、雜草、青苔和石頭的小徑
悲慟,隱隱約約在樹蔭中
手持她遺留下來的相機
也留下她握過的體溫
觀景器接目鏡,老是對不到焦點
ISO 太低,抑是太高
對不到焦點,眼睛穿過
她眼睛的對焦,按下快門

我爬上一粒厚重的石頭
一隻巨大的蜘蛛,等待著
在兩株菅芒花中,網住了

我識字
I am Literate

載著記憶的風,托住相機
畏懼它墜落,溺斃了回憶
的呼吸,前方傳來潺潺的
水聲

她坐在白色的沙發椅上
淚珠,沿著眼眶哭泣哽咽的說
「阿爹,請您為我找一位腦神經內科醫師」
小瀑布唱著,我想哭,
我想哭哭哭哭哭哭哭
陽光在水珠上跳躍
按不下快門
「阿爹,不是這樣對焦,不是這樣對焦」
抬頭看遠方的天空,有藍雲、有白雲……
她對我揮手手手手手手手手
喀擦一聲,小瀑布浮現她的身影
有一點孤獨的臉貌,坐在石頭上

她，躺在白色的床上
一再的坐起來，又躺下來
伸不出援救的手
拿起相機，向遠方對焦
快門，按不下去
——白色的床單，靜佳眠

D

她，活了　29歲
做為父親的我
給了她什麼
生活給了她什麼
生命給了她什麼

地球嘆了一口氣說
傾聽，一滴露水
夠了

我識字
I am Literate

傾聽,咚
露水一滴

夠了

2025/4/16　修

給女兒詩穎

心肝寶貝
——詩穎
你一定知道
阿爹喜歡買詩集
也盼望你喜歡讀詩

你誕生的那一天
阿爹想了一整天
想了整整一個晚上
心中浮懸著未來的畫面
長大之後　是一位女詩人
長大之後　是一位聰穎的女詩人

小時候
在書房讀書讀累了
阿爹想抱你　逗你
你總是嚎啕大哭
我是怪叔叔

我識字
I am Literate

我是大野狼
我是虎姑婆

小時候　生日到了
阿爹總會坐火車到台北中山北路的敦煌書局
購買進口的英文繪本送給你
你總是小心翼翼的收藏著

我買了一套彼得兔全集（Peter Rabbit）
發現你愛不釋手
時常自己一個人坐在地板上翻閱
讀得津津有味

小時候
阿爹忙著探索　愛麗絲夢遊奇境記
常常忘記

詩穎也是一本需要關懷的繪本

總是忘了邀你一同探險童話的國度

就讀實小一年級
阿爹就教你讀詩寫詩
　　「姊姊總是說我很吵
　　　天天一直東家長西家短的
　　　任何事情都有分
　　　我告訴她
　　　誰叫吵字
　　　是──
　　　少不了口呢」

讀向上國中時　　期待
讀西苑高中時　　期待
讀輔仁大學時　　期待
你會讀詩寫詩

我識字
I am Literate

輔仁大學畢業
準備到英國留學
你找到了自己的位置
自己申請學校
自己辦理出國手續
自己扛著大背包
在中港路搭乘統聯 Bus
自己坐飛機到英國 Newcastle 大學

畢業了　返回故鄉台中
自己又扛著大背包
站在門口按電鈴
你寫了一首〈我已經長大〉的詩
滋潤了全家人的心靈

2012 年 6 月 6 日
到榮總辦理住院治療
你又把詩寫在臉上

不畏懼癌細胞的吞噬

2013年2月17日晚上
你努力的想坐起來
一再努力的想坐起來
一再努力的……

詩是什麼
阿爹哀傷的讀懂了

你完成了唯一的一首詩
〈勇敢的野百合〉

我識字
I am Literate

為女兒禱告

天堂那裡
沒有高鐵吧
沒有飛機吧
沒有公車吧
沒有網路吧
可以禱告吧

「你什麼食物都要吃
　食物才願意把愛送給你」

「你要時常，坐夢回家」

阿爹，閉上眼睛
天堂變得好近

睜開眼睛，我仍然
不願意她上天堂

2018/12/30　修

蠶

悲傷孵化為蠶
飢餓,吃我的記憶
她,青春歲月

吃飽了,還是餓
又吃,我對她的思念、期盼……
有兩片大葉子
長了肺腺癌的葉子

吃一小片
咀嚼幾下
馬上吐絲
做了一個夢

夢見,她小時候
她把不想吃的東西,通通
丟到床底下

我識字
I am Literate

這不是夢
比真實還真實的
一張相片

是存在
也是不存在

2021/4/28

國家大事

早上
識字的老人
趕緊讀完報紙
國家大事,我吃完了

早上
不識字的老人
趕緊走到菜園澆水、拔草
國家大事,我做了

早上
躺在床上的老人
菲傭推他出去曬太陽
國家大事,我管不了

我識字
I am Literate

早上
在急診室的老人
等待上帝的關愛
國家大事,我放下了

早上
躺在棺木的老人
等待上天堂
國家大事,我不知道

早上
長眠在墳墓的老人
等待清明節那一天
國家大事,墓上的野草

吾鄉北斗

聽不見
百貨公司擁擠的人潮
聽得見
店仔頭的聊天
這是吾鄉的
  臉

鐵馬踩下去
叫不出來
這是吾鄉的
  身體

土土的土角厝
長不高
這是吾鄉的
  心

我識字
I am Literate

買不起
蜜絲佛陀的化妝品
買水果
請宮口的媽祖吃
這是吾鄉的
信仰

年輕人
嚮往
都市的天空
老年人
放不下
泥土的汗珠
守著列祖列宗的腳印

2019/05

風景

攝影家按下快門
拍照風景
不能沒有任何的想像
風景再現

畫家拿起彩筆
畫下風景
可以任意添加自己的想像
風景抽象
風景抽象的
也想要發掘風景
風景心中的風景

2018/2/6 修

我識字
I am Literate

作者簡介

　　蔡榮勇，1955年出生於台灣彰化縣北斗鎮，台中師專畢業。現為笠詩社社務兼編輯委員、台灣現代詩人協會理事、世界詩人組織（PPDM）會員。曾出版詩集《生命的美學》、《洗衣婦》及合集多種。2009年曾赴蒙古參加台蒙詩歌交流，2014年分別參加在古巴及智利舉行的國際詩歌節。

譯者簡介

　　戴茉莉（Emily Anna Deasy），愛爾蘭籍。西元 1995 至 2010 年居住台灣台北。愛爾蘭科克大學亞洲語言學系對外漢語學碩士畢業。目前與家庭居住加拿大卑詩省，就職小學老師以及翻譯。

我識字
I am Literate

英語篇

CONTENTS

75	I am Literate ·	我識字
79	Prayer ·	禱告
80	Sentiments of Taiwan ·	台灣的心事
81	Washer Woman ·	洗衣婦
82	Sugarcane Trains ·	五分車
84	I Am Still Learning ·	我還在學
86	The Fangyuan Seaside ·	芳苑海邊
87	A Long Time A Long Time ·	許久　許久
89	Catholic Church ·	天主教堂
90	Mazu Temple ·	媽祖廟
91	Read ·	讀
93	Illiterate Mother ·	不識字的母親
94	Father's Name ·	萬仔！萬仔！
95	Chicken Vendor ·	賣雞販
97	I Am More Fortunate Than Father ·	我比阿爸幸福
99	Silencing the Heart ·	靜下心來
101	Shoes ·	鞋
102	Taiwan Spirit ·	台灣精神
103	Awkward ·	尷尬
104	Who Will Be the Referee ·	誰當裁判
106	Self-portrait ·	自畫像
107	Sunflower ·	太陽花

109　The Washerwoman・洗衣婦
111　With Only Herself Left・剩下她自己
113　The Auditory Sense of Grief・悲慟的聽覺
121　For My Daughter Sherrie・給女兒詩穎
126　Praying for My Daughter・為女兒禱告
127　Silkworms・蠶
129　Major National Affairs・國家大事
131　My Hometown Beidou・吾鄉北斗
133　Landscape・風景

134　About the Poet・作者簡介
135　About the Translator・譯者簡介

I am Literate

Father lost his father
When he was very, very young
Never tasted the flavor of schooling

Father opened wide the eyes of life
And relied on his hands and feet
To raise us

I am literate
I realized that father
Under the Kuomintang's emphasis of Chinese
Felt self-pity, held back, and lived his days hidden in a corner

I am literate
I realized that father
Was labeled as poor
A rushed joy at a meal
With time enough to worry for the next

我識字
I am Literate

I am literate
I could not escape the Kuomintang
Their haughty rule
Each meal was still one struggle after the next
Afraid to take rest even briefly as the moon and sun brushed shoulders

I am literate
I had my child learn English and Japanese
That she could look further than the Taiwan Straight
She sat in a university classroom in England
In class

I am literate
My child got sick
Before my very eyes she went up to heaven
My hands shriveled, and my soul dried up
My days are out-of-focus images

I am literate
And I cannot see God
I want to say to God
My daughter was the hope
Of my whole life

It was not easy
For a small yellow flower to bloom forth
from a rock weighed down by the Kuomintang rule
Before it had a chance to show its face in the breeze
It was blown down

I am literate
Yet cannot find
A plane that I can take up to heaven
I scrub my sorrow with poetry
And become more sorrowful

我識字
I am Literate

I am literate
And the world is the same
It does not hold on to
Any of my footsteps
A single withered leaf that falls

Prayer

Standing on the sandbank
Rows of waterbirds
Silently pray
"When hungry, that I may
get fresh little fish to eat"

Amen

Wings flap
They dip down to the water's surface
Scooping up the little fish
Then to sleep with one leg up
Welcoming good dreams that come with the dark night

我識字
I am Literate

Sentiments of Taiwan

Unable to say the name of our own country

Taiwan

Unable to read that which was passed down from our ancestors

Culture

Not allowed to use the language that mother spoke in

To read   to speak   to write

How   are we supposed to be

Visionaries

   And be

      Forward-looking

Washer Woman

The sky opens up its drowsy eyes
And hurries to   take off
Youth is pawned to dirty clothes
Together with heart and soul
Pawned away as well

A spoonful of laundry detergent
A basin of wet clothes
Waiting   for the calling of the wind
Waiting   for a love letter from the sunshine
Waiting   for the kindness of a banknote

Fingertips   overworked
A dog's open mouth
Mimicking lightning   SOS
I don't want to be poor
I don't want to be poor

我識字
I am Literate

Sugarcane Trains

Taking the train   each time I go back home
I can only take it to Yuanlin
Then switch to Taiwan Transport Bus to get back to Beidou
My eyes cannot help but turn toward
The sugarcane trains of my youth
Beishicha Station was in front of my house

Whenever the train would pull into the station
You would hear the whistle sound 'bu, bu, bu'
That was the train carrying sugarcane
If you heard a sighing sound
That was the train carrying passengers

Now Taiwan Sugar Corp's sugar-making has declined
The sugarcane trains decommissioned, the train stations sold
The land bulldozed, and people fight to buy it
To build unregulated buildings to rent out

The feeling of home

Is like the weeds before my eyes ──

Lonely Isolated

我識字
I am Literate

I Am Still Learning

A cluster of green seedlings
Under the sun
A steady green

A cluster of green seedlings
Under the sun
A green visage

A cluster of green seedlings
Under the sun
A green smile

A cluster of green seedlings
Under the sun
Searching for green sayings

Tired of searching
The sun says heatedly
It is time to rest

The Autumn breeze has bought
A new dictionary of sayings
And gifted it to the seedlings

The seedlings say politely
I am still learning
Thank you

我識字
I am Literate

The Fangyuan Seaside

The beach at the Fangyuan Seaside is a stretch of empty silence
The small and muddy country roads
A yellow cow passes through the soul of the sea breeze
Pulling the cart with a vertical sort of parallel
Step on the sand   a footprint
A footprint which chases the setting sun

A shadow of a person that is more familiar than the seaside
She passes by the seaside of dreams
The gazing sunset   the lingering afterglow
She comes close to me, comes in to me
Leaps into the soul   golden rabbit and silver frog[1]
Their window to the moon

---

[1]   From ancient folklore that depicts a golden rabbit and silver frog that live on the moon.

A Long Time A Long Time

A long time   A long time
Worshiping with father   Ancestors that I have seen before
A long time   A long time
Worshiping with father   Ancestors that I have not seen before
A long time   A long time
Worshiping with father   Ancestors that father has not seen before

Worshiping ancestors   Ancestor's silhouette
The silhouette of ancestor's ancestors   Worship
The silhouette of ancestor's ancestors

After a hundred days
Father became a silhouette of an ancestor
Remember to worship   on the first and fifteenth day of the Lunar calendar

I got used to looking at father's perspiring eyes
I am unaccustomed to the eyes in father's memorial portrait

我識字
I am Literate

It is a small book of history
Preserving   father's countless
Eyes

Three sticks of incense in my hands
Accustomed to father's eyes
My eyes
Are timid and fearful

The ancestors
Must have something they wish to say
But   they cannot be heard
The intense flames from burning gold paper
I see
Father's eyes
Glowing with what seems like an intense fire

Catholic Church

Walk into the church
A lingering kneel with the right knee
Lightly make the sign of the cross with the right hand
Sit down, listening
The priest preaches in warm Taiwanese

My spirit calms
Like the Jade Mountain of Taiwan
Mother's berating words
Like the dark clouds above
Float away

Edited on Jan 17th, 2013

我識字
I am Literate

Mazu Temple

Mother's heart is troubled
She buys a few pieces of fruit
She buys a box of biscuits
She buys a bunch of incense
She buys a stack of paper money
And goes to Mazu at the temple
To tell Mazu, to plead
For good health and success in studies

After coming home
I was the happiest
I had fruit to eat
Biscuits to eat

On mother's face
There are still a few grey clouds
Lingering on her forehead

Read

Only able to say a few words of Chinese
Mother
In the land of words
Her eyes cannot find
The key

Working   Reading daily
Tired of reading   Read some more
The children
Tired of reading   Eyes of dreams
Keep on reading
Tired of reading   Read the dreams
Of the children

The children also wrote a book
One she loves to read
Think   Take it out

我識字
I am Literate

It cannot be taken out
Read it to them
"It's too long"
She says

Illiterate Mother

Illiterate mother
The expression on everyone's face
Are lines of the poem that move her

Her daily work
The prose she must read

Chatting with people
The novels she loves to read

The loving heart for her children
Philosophy that she never tires of reading

She does not know
That she is for her children
An encyclopedia that they love to read

我識字
I am Literate

Father's Name

After father passed away
Mother held two 50 yuan coins in her hands
Shouting out father's nickname   again and again
"Darling! My darling!
Do you approve
If I do it this way?"

After losing a sixty-year-long partner
Mother's   loneliness
Was colder than the snow
Of the Arctic

The care of her children
Could not mend
Mother's heart
Just a piece of jade, falling to the floor

Chicken Vendor

A pair of hands
A pair of feet
A hardworking heart
Carrying the wellbeing of a family of six

A bicycle carries
A basket of chickens
Through the streets and alleyways
All over the village
Calling out
"Delicious and affordable local chicken!"
"Delicious and affordable local chicken!"

Laying on the bed   watching
This film
Tears become mosquitoes
Buzzing at the ears

我識字
I am Literate

The sunshine shouts brightly by the window
"Get up!"
"The sun is high in the sky!"
The sunshine does not know
How sweet is it to watch like this

I Am More Fortunate Than Father

I was born in 1955
I am more fortunate than father
Father would be by my side   reminding me
   Planting bananas   Harvesting bananas

Father, who did not have a father to remind him
Did not know how to be a father
Often silent like a stone
The banana leaf green like jade

Father went up to heaven
It seems more real than when he was alive
I would go back to visit him when he was alive
The road has become wider now that he is in heaven

我識字
I am Literate

I am more fortunate than father

Father would be by my side   reminding me

Father is up in heaven

I can truly remember

                                              Edited on Jan 9th, 2019

Silencing the Heart

Starting tomorrow   I will open a school
Leaving the classrooms   leaving the sports track
Leaving the sweet and innocent students
Silencing the heart   remembering Taichung University
Experimental Elementary School [1]

Starting tomorrow   I will walk toward the countryside
And learn from the farmers how to plant the rice paddies
Learn from the sparrows how it feels to watch the rice grow
Silencing the heart   remembering Taichung University
Experimental Elementary School

Starting tomorrow   I will walk toward the fishing villages
And learn from the fishermen how to catch fish
Learn from the seagulls the joy of flying
Silencing the heart   remembering Taichung University
Experimental Elementary School

我識字
I am Literate

Starting tomorrow　　I will walk toward the mountains
And learn from the indigenous people how to listen to the silence
Learn from the thousand-year sacred tree the silence of loneliness
Silencing the heart　　remembering Taichung University
Experimental Elementary School

Starting tomorrow　　I will walk toward myself
Walk toward the utopia of my own life
Converse and even debate with life
Silencing the heart　　remembering Taichung University
Experimental Elementary School

¹ Taichung University Experimental Elementary School is a school where the poet taught.

Shoes

Women wear shoes
Not to   write essays for men to   read
Nor to   write stories for men to   read
But instead   to write a short poem for youth to read

Women buy shoes
Perhaps to switch up the man
Or to commit infidelity
Maybe to fall into the net of desire

The shoes that sit on the shelf
Their mouths   open like an O
Are they tired
Or do they have something to say

我識字
I am Literate

Taiwan Spirit

In elementary, junior high school, and teaching school   The history textbooks were full of Chinese history
In every dynasty the emperor was either useless or violent to another
Then the courageous revolted and won the dragon robe
Good people, bad people, like two lines, stringing the five thousand years of history together

In Taiwanese history Zheng Chenggong's driving out of the Dutch is often mentioned
And there are constant praises for how great Chiang Kai-shek was
And the reason why the mainland was lost is a hazy fog

Our illiterate parents learned the Taiwan spirit
They worked hard all their lives, and treated people with kindness and warmth
Living frugally and simply

2001.10.20
2019.05.09

Awkward

The sacred decree of Chiang Kai-shek
Anti-communism and anti-Russia
Written on your arm   with a needle
Anti-communism and anti-Russia   Missing home

Lee Teng-hui said
End the martial law
Veterans can go home

On the arm
Green coloured words, anti-communism and anti-Russia
In the operating theatre   it tells the story
Of my hometown
To the little flower   in the bottle

我識字
I am Literate

Who Will Be the Referee

In elementary school
The teacher kept reminding us
"Anti-communism and anti-Russia"

In junior high school
The teacher kept reminding us
"Don't forget the motherland"

In teaching school
The teacher kept reminding us
"Stay calm under pressure"

When I was teaching
President Chiang Ching-kuo said
I am a Taiwanese person too

When I got married
President Lee Teng-hui declared
The end of martial law

Heading into my middle-age years
The knots of China and the knots of Taiwan
Were in a tug-of-war

Who will be the referee
Is it the sun
Who has climbed so high

我識字
I am Literate

Self-portrait

Retired
And no longer a teacher
As I walk on the road I am like the trees on the roadside
Very few people   lift their head to look at you

Not able to drive
I like to take trains and observe the view
Not a rich person
I play some badminton, sweat a bit
Sometimes   I will read some poetry collections
Sometimes   I will plant some flowers or trees
Sometimes   I will write poetry or draw

Life
Is lived just like this
Trying
To ground my soul deeply
On the Taiwanese soil that nurtured me

2006.11.25 Edited

Sunflower

Sunflower   Awakens
The spirit of the Wild Lily Student Movement
Searching for the window where Taiwan exists

The full bloom of the sunflower
The blood flower of Cheng Nan-jung's self-immolation
The blood flower of Chan I-hua's self-immolation

The sun is not fearful of the black box trade agreement
Holding the sunflower up high
Waiting for the daylight's shining rays

The sunflower   illuminates   the chairman of Acer
He says "If the trade agreement doesn't pass, there will be no hope for Taiwan's industry!"

The sunflower   illuminates   the chairman of the E-United Group

我識字
I am Literate

He says　　that he will temporarily postpone all investment in Taiwan

The sunflower　　illuminates　　the chairman of Taiwan Plastics
He says　　if this keeps going on, we might not even get the 15K!

The sunflower　　illuminates　　the founder of Delta Electronics
He says　　Taiwan is at risk of being sidelined

The cloud of sunflower　　drives away
The corruption of Ma's government

The global network of the sunflower
Scares away the conversation of sticks and clubs

2019/4/18 Edited

The Washerwoman

The poet Shiang-hua Chang, "*A Red Sweater*"
Soft, tough
Warmth, turns into a nagging reminder

The poet Duo Si, "*Washing Clothes*"
Ambition shortens inch by inch
But love and care keep growing piece by piece

Mother is not a poet, but is *The Washerwoman*
In the early morning of a cold day
With both hands on the washboard
Transforming the dirty clothes of many houses
Into clean

Cleanliness is written on her cracking fingertips
With drips of blood

我識字
I am Literate

Note: I remember that in grade five and six of elementary school, my afterschool tuition was five thousand yuan each month. In order to pay the tuition, mother humbly washed the clothes of some rich families that lived nearby, earning five thousand yuan every month. Whenever I think of this situation, my tears have nowhere to hide. The women of those wealthy houses who lacked empathy would often throw an immeasurable amount of laundry at my mother to wash.

2019/1/26 Edited

With Only Herself Left

Mother cannot speak Mandarin
Mother cannot speak Hakka
Mother cannot speak indigenous languages
Mother cannot read the newspaper
She can look at the world with her eyes
She can listen to the world with her ears
She can read the world with her soul

Her world cannot be expanded by books
Allowing her to walk in worlds unknown

She uses the language told to her by her mother
She reads the world with her eyes
She does not have to use a dictionary, because there are no words

After father passed away
She got even older
Her world got smaller and smaller

我識字
I am Literate

With only herself left

Loneliness

2018/2/13
2021/4/28 Edited

The Auditory Sense of Grief

> You are not a drop in the ocean. You are the entire ocean in a drop. – Rumi

Overture

She became a legend, finally able to fly everywhere like a sparrow. Finding no branch to rest, she falls into my sadness, leaving a deep dent.

A

Listen, sad auditory sense of sadness
Longing more than the time alive
Time alive more than the longing
I follow the longing and return to her childhood years
And wipe off the dirt under the soles of her shoes

我識字
I am Literate

With each step, looking back subtly
Each glance back, the heart and soul are glass shattered all over the floor
She is the most important subject
I collect verbs from all over
Slowly, mending the shattered heart and soul

With each step, some verbs have to be discarded
Arriving at the childhood years, a picture book is propped up ahead
An eye-catching title, *You Are a Book of Life*

She, in between the two words,
Life and death, disappeared into another word
I will read death with life, and find the dwelling place of death.

B

The language of death is like a squid

When it meets with a strong enemy, it constantly

Spits out black ink, the giant belly of the ocean

Feels nothing at all, and yet

Waves come and go, the fishermen

Keep catching fish, the sea breeze

Opens its wide wings

Howling, the fishing boat bobs up and down

Steering toward the coast, with the fisherman's full boat of fish

The words of life, are written again and again

Race toward the fish market, race toward every

Consumer's belly

The language of death is like a withered shinboku tree

Unable to grow green buds

Because the roots are already rotted

The living shinboku tree

With leaves green and lush

The wrinkles of the bark are wrinkles of the years

我識字
I am Literate

The wind blows and it moves
The birds are willing to come to rest and sing

The withered shinboku tree   waits silently
For the cutting of the axe
To make chairs, tables, carvings
She is dead, these three words
Time cannot recall
The sun has long forgotten
The moon still shines on her window
Her shadow is the same as the moon
In front of her bed   the moonlight   cannot
Lift up the head   to look at the bright moon

Missing her
I lift my head to look at the bright moon

C

She, is in heaven now
Following the twists and turns of this sentence
True or false, thorns that choke one another
The little path with trees, weeds, moss and rocks
Grief, can be seen vaguely in the shadows of the trees
With the camera she left behind in my hand
Along with the heat of her grip
The viewfinder and the lens, always hard to focus
ISO too low, or is it too high
Cannot find the focus, my eyes look through
The focus of her eyes, press the shutter down

I climb onto a big rock
A huge spider, waits
In between two swan flowers, the web is set

我識字
I am Literate

The wind that carries memories, holds on to the camera
Afraid that it will fall, and drown the memories
Of their breath, babbling from ahead
The sound of water

She sits on a white sofa
Tears, fall down her face as she sobs and says
"Dad, please find a neurologist for me."
The little waterfall sings, I want to cry,
I want to cry cry cry cry cry cry cry
The sunshine dances on the water droplets
Cannot press the shutter button down
"Dad, that's not how you focus, that's not how you focus."
I lift my eyes to look at the faraway sky, blue clouds, white clouds…
She waves at me with her hand hand hand hand hand hand hand hand hand
One click, and her silhouette appears in the little waterfall,
Her face is a little lonely, sitting on a rock

She, lays on a white bed,

Keeps sitting up, then laying back down

Can't reach out a saving hand   Take up the camera, focusing on faraway,

Shutter, can't click

------ white sheets, sleep well and in peace

D

She, lived for 29 years

I, as her father

What have I given her

What has life given her

What has life given her

The earth lets out a sigh and says

Listen, a dewdrop

Is enough

我識字
I am Literate

Listen, drop!
A drop of dew

Enough

2021/4/28 Edited

For My Daughter Sherrie

My darling sweetheart
-------- Sherrie
You surely know
That Dad likes to buy poetry collections
And hoped you would like to read poems

The day you were born
Dad thought the whole day
And through the whole night
And a vison of the future showed up in my heart
When you grew up   you would be a female poet
When you grew up   you would be an intelligent female poet

When you were young
And tired of reading in the study
Dad would want to hug you and play with you
And you would always howl and cry
I was the strange uncle

我識字
I am Literate

I was the big bad wolf
I was Aunt Tiger

When you were young   and your birthday arrived
Dad would take a train to Chung Shan North Road in Taipei, to
Caves Books
And purchase imported English picture books for you
You would always carefully collect them

I bought the full collection of Peter Rabbit
And found that you loved them and could not put them down
Often sitting alone on the floor paging through them
Relishing the reading

When you were young
Dad was busy exploring   Alice in Wonderland
Often forgetting

That Sherrie was also a picture book that needed care

Always forgetting to invite you along to explore the lands of fairy tales

When you went to grade one at the experimental school
Dad taught you to read and write poetry
> **"Sister always says I'm so noisy**
> **Always gossiping about this and that**
> **Something to say about everything**
> **I told her**
> **Whose fault is it that the word for noisy**
> **Is one that**
> **Requires a mouth**[1]

When you went to Xiangshang Junior High School   I anticipated
When you went to Shiyuan Senior High School   I anticipated
When you went to Fu Jen University   I anticipated
That you would read and write poetry

我識字
I am Literate

When you graduated from Fu Jen University
And were preparing to study abroad in England
You found your own place
And applied for school yourself
Handled the paperwork to leave the country yourself
Carried a big backpack yourself
You took a Tonglian Bus from Taichung Port Road
To take the plane by yourself to Newcastle University

After you graduated   You returned to your hometown in Taichung
Carrying a big backpack again
And you stood at the doorway and pressed the doorbell
You wrote a poem called *I Am Grown Up Now*
That nourished the souls of your family members

June 6th, 2012
Went to Veteran's General Hospital to be admitted for treatment

You wrote another poem on your face
That you did not fear the engulfing cancer cells

Nighttime of February 17th, 2013
You worked hard at trying to sit up
Again and again trying to sit up
Again and again…

What is a poem
Dad finally understands with his sad heart

You completed the one and only poem
Courageous Wild Lily

---

[1] Translator's note: the Chinese character for noisy is 吵, and the character for mouth is 口. If you look at the character for noisy, you can see that there is a character for mouth on the left side.

我識字
I am Literate

Praying for My Daughter

Up there in heaven
Surely there is no high-speed railway
Surely there are no airplanes
Surely there are no buses
Surely there is no internet
You must be able to pray

"You have to eat every kind of food
For the food to be willing to give you love"

"You have to ride your dreams and visit home, often"

Dad, close your eyes
Heaven becomes so close

Open your eyes, I am still
Unwilling for her to be in heaven

2018/12/30 Edited

Silkworms

Sadness hatches into silkworms

Hungry, eating my memories

She, in her youth

Ate her fill, and would still be hungry

Eat again, my memories of her, expectations…

There are two big leaves

Leaves that have grown lung adenocarcinoma

Eat a little leaf

Chew a few times

Spit out silk immediately

Dreaming a dream

In my dream I see her, when she was young

She would throw the food she did not want to eat, all of it

Under her bed

我識字
I am Literate

This is not a dream
It is more real than reality
A photograph

It is existence
And is also nonexistence

2021/4/28 Edited

Major National Affairs

Morning
The literate old person
Reads the newspaper hurriedly
Major national affairs, I have finished eating

Morning
The illiterate old person
Hurriedly goes to the garden to water and weed it
Major national affairs, I have completed them

Morning
The old person who lies on the bed
The maid from the Philippines pushes them out to the sunshine
Major national affairs, I cannot care about them

我識字
I am Literate

Morning

The old person in the emergency room

Waiting for the love of God

Major national affairs, I have let go

Morning

The old person lying in the coffin

Waiting to go to heaven

Major national affairs, I do not know

Morning

The old person in the cemetery in a long slumber

Waiting for the day of tomb-sweeping

Major national affairs, the weeds on the grave

My Hometown Beidou

I cannot hear
The bustling waves of people in the department store
I can hear
The chatting of the shopkeepers
This is my hometown's
Face

I ride my bike
It cannot speak
This is my hometown's
Body

The muddy mud dwellings
Cannot grow taller
This is my hometown's
Heart

我識字
I am Literate

I cannot afford
Max Factor cosmetics
I buy some fruit
To give to the Mazu by the temple entrance
This is my hometown's
Faith

Young people
Wish for
The city sky
Old people
Cannot set down
The sweat of the earth
And guard the footprints of all our ancestors

2019.05 Edited

Landscape

The photographer presses down the shutter
Takes a picture of the landscape
It cannot be without any imagination
The landscape is shown again

The artist picks up their colors
And draws a picture of the landscape
They can add anything they like from their imagination
An abstract landscape

The landscape abstractly
Wants to discover the landscape
The landscape in the heart of the landscape

2018/2/6 Edited

我識字
I am Literate

About the Poet

     Tsai Jung-Yung was born in Beidou, Changhua County, Taiwan in 1955. After graduating from Taichung Teachers' College, He went to Mongolia on the poetry exchange between Taiwan and Mongolia in 2009. He attended International Poetry Festivals respectively in Cuba and Chile in 2014.He is currently an editing member of Li Poetry Group, a director in Taiwan Modern Poets' Association, and a member of PPDM.

About the Translator

Emily Anna Deasy is from Cork, Ireland, and lived in Taipei, Taiwan from 1995 to 2010. She received her master's degree in TCSOL (Teaching Chinese to Speakers of Other Languages) from University College Cork, Ireland, and currently resides with her family in British Columbia, Canada, where she works as a translator and elementary school teacher.

我識字
I am Literate

語言文學類 PG3186 台灣詩叢25

我識字 I am Literate
——蔡榮勇漢英雙語詩集

作　　者 / 蔡榮勇（Tsai Jung-yung）
譯　　者 / 戴茉莉（Emily Anna Deasy）
叢書策畫 / 李魁賢（Lee Kuei-shien）
責任編輯 / 吳霽恆
圖文排版 / 黃莉珊
封面設計 / 嚴若綾

出版策劃 / 秀威資訊科技股份有限公司
法律顧問 / 毛國樑　律師
製作發行 / 秀威資訊科技股份有限公司
　　　　　114台北市內湖區瑞光路76巷65號1樓
　　　　　電話：+886-2-2796-3638　傳真：+886-2-2796-1377
　　　　　http://www.showwe.com.tw
劃撥帳號 / 19563868　戶名：秀威資訊科技股份有限公司
　　　　　讀者服務信箱：service@showwe.com.tw
展售門市 / 國家書店（松江門市）
　　　　　104台北市中山區松江路209號1樓
　　　　　電話：+886-2-2518-0207　傳真：+886-2-2518-0778
網路訂購 / 秀威網路書店：https://store.showwe.tw
　　　　　國家網路書店：https://www.govbooks.com.tw
經　　銷 / 聯合發行股份有限公司
　　　　　231新北市新店區寶橋路235巷6弄6號4F
　　　　　電話：+886-2-2917-8022　傳真：+886-2-2915-6275

2025年7月　BOD一版
定價：280元
版權所有　翻印必究
本書如有缺頁、破損或裝訂錯誤，請寄回更換

Copyright©2025 by Showwe Information Co., Ltd.
Printed in Taiwan
All Rights Reserved

讀者回函卡

國家圖書館出版品預行編目

我識字 I am literate：蔡榮勇漢英雙語詩集 / 蔡榮勇著；Emily Anna Deasy譯. -- 一版. -- 臺北市：秀威資訊科技股份有限公司, 2025.07
　面；　公分. -- (語言文學類；PG3186)(台灣詩叢；25)
　中英對照
　BOD版
　ISBN 978-626-7511-92-3(平裝)

863.51　　　　　　　　　　　114006735